Little Monkey
Says Good Night

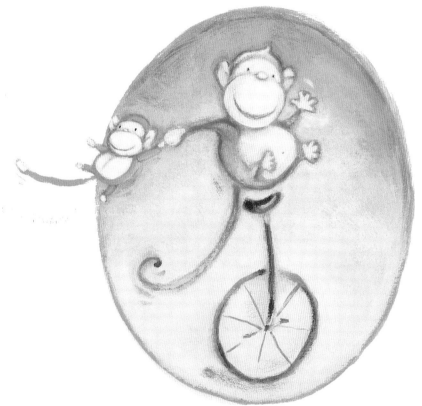

by Ann Whitford Paul ★ Pictures by David Walker

Melanie Kroupa Books
Farrar, Straus and Giroux ★ New York

For Alan,
the original Little Monkey
—A.W.P.

For Sydney,
my first "good night" girl
—D.W.

Text copyright © 2003 by Ann Whitford Paul
Illustrations copyright © 2003 by David Walker
All rights reserved
Distributed in Canada by Douglas & McIntyre Ltd.
Color separations by Chroma Graphics PTE Ltd.
Printed and bound in the United States of America by Phoenix Color Corporation
Designed by Jennifer Browne
First edition, 2003
3 5 7 9 10 8 6 4 2

Library of Congress Cataloging-in-Publication Data
Paul, Ann Whitford.
   Little monkey says good night / by Ann Whitford Paul ; pictures by David Walker.
       p.   cm.
   Summary: When Little Monkey says good night to the performers in the big top tent, he
creates a circus act of his own.
   ISBN 0-374-34609-7
   [1. Monkeys—Fiction.   2. Circus—Fiction.   3. Bedtime—Fiction.]   I. Walker, David, ill.
II.   Title.

PZ7.P278338 Li 2002
[E]—dc21
                                                                                    2001038396

"Come, Little Monkey," Papa Monkey says. "The sky is dark. The moon is high. It's time for bed."
Little Monkey shakes his head. "First I need to say good night."

He scampers to the Big Top tent.
"Come back," calls Papa.

But Little Monkey jumps

BOING!

into Ringmaster's spotlight. "Good night, Ringmaster."
Ringmaster tips his tall top hat and sweeps Little Monkey

SWISH!

through Poodle's hoops.

"Good night, Poodle."

"Woof! Woof!"

Little Monkey takes a big step back . . .

CLUNK!

and tumbles into a small red car.
"Good night, Bozo. Good night,
Buttons. Good night, Bumbles."
The clowns somersault out and

BUMP!

Little Monkey up onto Horse.
"Good night, Horse."
Horse rears high. Little Monkey slides

right onto Lion's back.
"Good night, Lion."
"GRRRRRRRRR!"

Little Monkey runs away

THUMP!

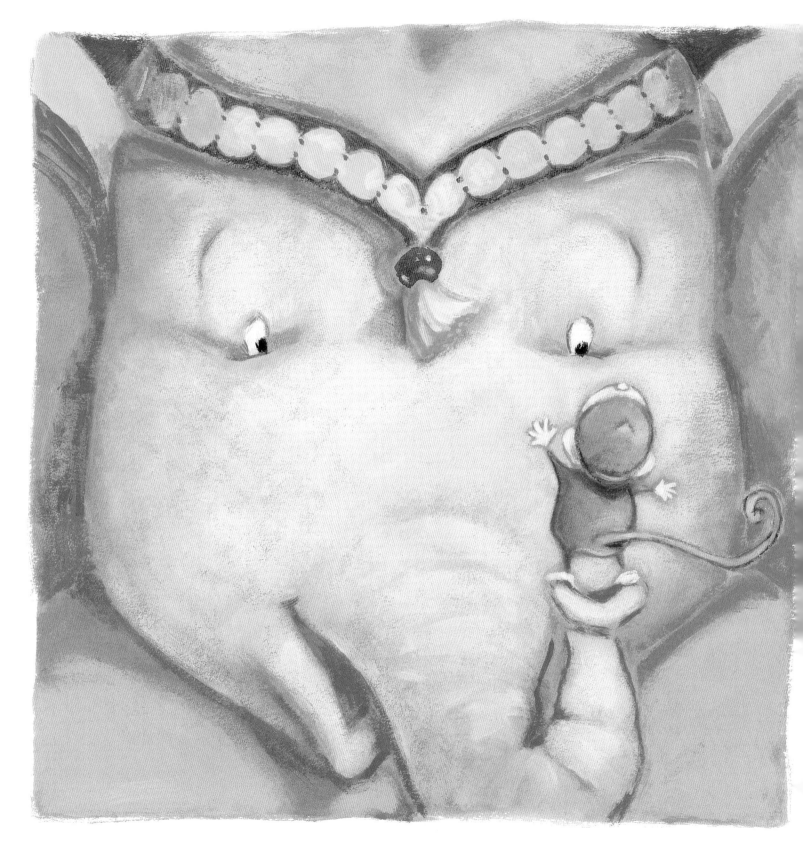

into Elephant.

"Good night, Elephant."

Elephant scoops Little Monkey up

onto Strongman's barbells.
"Good night, Strongman."

WOBBLE

Little Monkey dashes into the bandstand.
"Good night, Band!"

Rat-a-tat! Ring-a-ding! Toot-a-toot-TOOT!

The musicians chase Little Monkey

Juggler's plates go

BOUNCITY . . .

BOUNCITY . . .

BOUNCITY!

"Good night, Juggler!"

Up . . . and up . . . and up
Little Monkey climbs.

"Come down!" shouts Papa.
"Come down!" shout the clowns
and Strongman and Juggler.
But Little Monkey leaps

right into Mama's arms.
"Good night, Mama."

Then . . .

FLIP!

FLIP!

FLIP!

down to Papa.
"Good night, Papa."

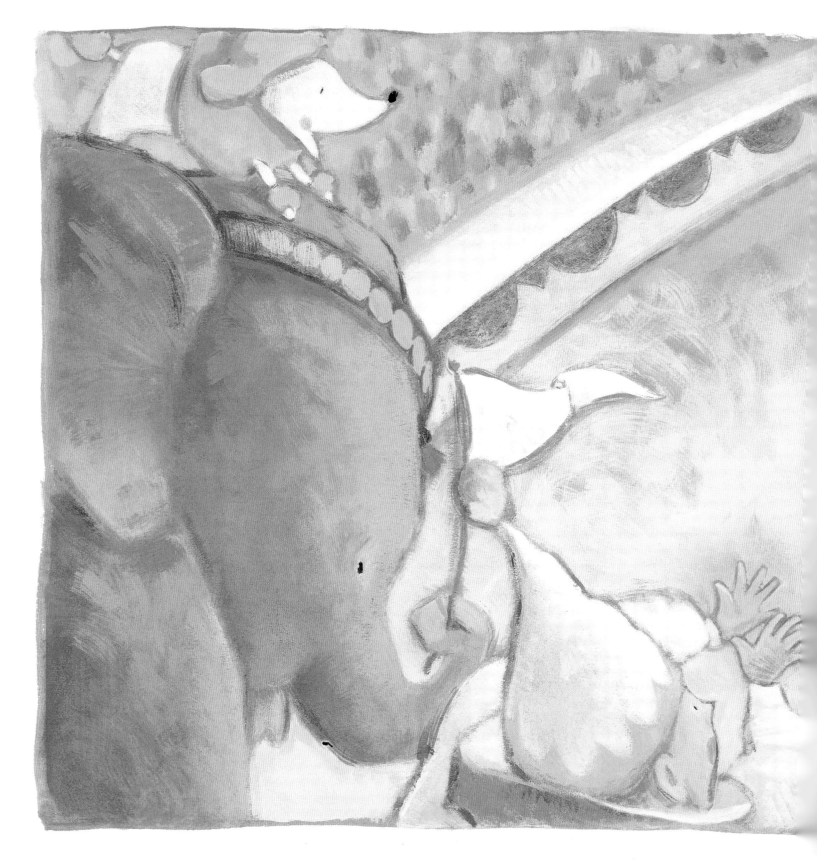

The crowd claps. They cheer.
And Little Monkey waves.
"Good night, everybody."
"Now," Papa says, "no more
good nights!"
"Just one more," says Little
Monkey . . .

"Good night, Me!"